SORI'S HARVEST MOON DAY

A Story of Korea

Written and illustrated
by Lee, Uk-Bae

Soundprints
Where Children Discover...

Illustrations copyright © 1995 Lee, Uk-Bae.
Translation copyright 1999 © Trudy Corporation, 353 Main Avenue, Norwalk, CT 06851.
Book copyright © 1999 Trudy Corporation.

Soundprints is a division of Trudy Corporation, Norwalk, Connecticut.

First English language edition 1999.
Book design: Scott Findlay
Editor: Judy Gitenstein

10 9 8 7 6 5 4 3 2 1
Printed in Hong Kong

Originally published in Korea as *Sori's Chu-Suk* by Gilbut Children Publishing Company 1995.
Sori's Harvest Moon Day published by arrangement with Gilbut Children Publishing Company.

Library of Congress Cataloging-in-Publication Data

Yi, Ŏk-pae.
[Sor-i ŭi ch' usŏk iyagi. English]
    Sori's harvest moon day : a story of Korea / written and illustrated by Lee, Uk-Bae.
        p.   cm.
    Summary: As she travels from the city to her grandmother's village, a young girl looks forward to her family's celebration of Chu-Suk, the harvest moon festival.
    ISBN 1-56899-687-X (hardcover) — ISBN 1-56899-688-8 (pbk)
    [1. Grandmothers—Fiction. 2. Festivals—Fiction. 3. Korea—Fiction.]   I. Title.
PZ7.Y525So   1999   98-51871
[E]—dc21   CIP
                                                                                  AC

SORI'S
HARVEST MOON DAY

A Story of Korea

Written and illustrated
by Lee, Uk-Bae

4

Everyone in the city is busy. Chu-Suk,
the Harvest Moon Festival, is only two days away.

Sori, her parents, and her little brother are up very
early to take a bus to Grandma's house. When they arrive
at the bus station, they must wait at the end of a long line.

The highway is very crowded, too. Many people are
leaving the city for their hometowns.

The trip takes almost all day.

When they arrive, the big guardian tree of the village is there to greet them. Sori and her parents place rocks beside the tree and pray for good health for their family.

"Grandma!" Sori's grandmother has come out to greet them.

13

Sori is happy to see her cousins and her aunts and uncles. Grandma's house is filled with laughter and activity—and the aroma of delicious food.

14

15

"Look, the moon is full," Sori says. The Harvest Moon Festival is a time to say thank-you for all the good fortune of the last year.

17

Today is Chu-Suk, Harvest Moon Day. Everyone gets up early for Cha-Rye, the service to remember family ancestors. The dishes are made with newly-harvested rice and fruit.

Later, everyone will pay a visit to the graves of their ancestors.

18

19

Sori, her father, and her cousins hear the sounds
of Pung-Mul, the Folk Festival. They join the parade.

農者天下之大本

今

21

The whole village dances
hand-in-hand, making circles as round as
the full moon.

22

Kang-kang-sul-lae lasts late into the night.

23

The next day, it is time to go home.
Grandma prepares bundles of food for
everyone to take home with them.

25

"Bye-bye, Grandma," Sori calls from the bus.
"Bye-bye, everyone! I will miss you all."

The family arrives home very late that night. Sori is already dreaming of next year's Harvest Moon Festival and her family's visit to Grandma's.

28

29

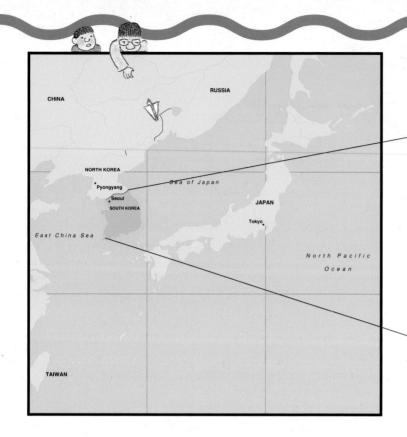

SOUTH KOREA

Seoul

Incheon

Taejeon

Taegu

Pusan

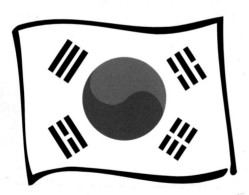

About Korea

Korea is a country located in the northeastern part of Asia, the largest continent in the world. Korea is a peninsula, which means that it is surrounded on three sides by water. Most of the country is mountainous.

Korea is divided into two parts: North and South Korea. The capital of South Korea, known as the Republic of Korea, is Seoul. The language, known as Korean, has an alphabet called Han-gul, which has ten vowels and fourteen consonants.

The population of Korea is 46 million.

About the Harvest Moon Festival

The Harvest Moon Festival always falls on the fifteenth day of the eighth moon, using the lunar calendar, or approximately October 4–6 in the solar calendar. The words *Chu-Suk* mean "the autumn set." This is harvest time in Korea. The Festival is very much like the American holiday Thanksgiving. In Korea, the Harvest Moon Festival is also a time to remember one's ancestors. People visit their hometowns—the place where their ancestors are buried—to pay their respects. Today in Korea, many people live and work in the cities. Their hometowns are usually in the countryside, in towns and villages very much like the one Sori visits with her family.

During Chu-Suk, or Hahn-ga-wi, as it is also called, the weather is usually perfect, and the food and other materials are more abundant than any other time of the year. Korean people eagerly await the time of year when the newly-harvested grains, "lumpy pumpkins," and other traditional foods are prepared by their mothers and fathers. The bundles that Sori's grandmother has lovingly presented for Sori to take back home with her are part of a time-honored tradition. For, as it says on the banner carried by one of the Pung-Mul players found in the illustration on page 21, *Nong-ja-chun-ha-ji-dae-bon*, which means "We farmers are the very root of the world."

You can find out more about Korean culture and customs by visiting your local library.

Here are some words that you will find spoken in Korea today:

Ahn-nyong-hi geh-seyo! (an-nyong-hi geh sey-ō): Good-bye! (Used especially with older people.)

borumdahl (bor-um-dal'): The full moon.

cham-gi-rum (cham'-gi-rum): Sesame oil.

dahl (dal): Moon.

gahm (gām): A persimmon.

halmoni (hal'-mun-i): Grandma.

nulgun hobak (nul'-gun hoh bahk): An old pumpkin, and so it is called a "lumpy pumpkin."

oak-su-suh (ohk'-su-suh): Corn.

ssahl (sal): Rice.